the VERY WORST ever

Go for the GOLD

BY ANDY NONAMUS
ILLUSTRATED BY AMY JINDRA

LITTLE SIMON
NEW YORK   LONDON   TORONTO   SYDNEY   NEW DELHI

If you purchased this book without a cover, you should be aware that this book is stolen property. It was reported as "unsold and destroyed" to the publisher, and neither the author nor the publisher has received any payment for this "stripped book."

This book is a work of fiction. Any references to historical events, real people, or real places are used fictitiously. Other names, characters, places, and events are products of the author's imagination, and any resemblance to actual events or places or persons, living or dead, is entirely coincidental.

LITTLE SIMON
An imprint of Simon & Schuster Children's Publishing Division
1230 Avenue of the Americas, New York, New York 10020
First Little Simon paperback edition November 2024
Copyright © 2024 by Simon & Schuster, LLC
Also available in a Little Simon hardcover edition.
All rights reserved, including the right of reproduction in whole or in part in any form.
LITTLE SIMON is a registered trademark of Simon & Schuster, LLC, and associated colophon is a trademark of Simon & Schuster, LLC.
Simon & Schuster: Celebrating 100 Years of Publishing in 2024
For information about special discounts for bulk purchases, please contact Simon & Schuster Special Sales at 1-866-506-1949 or business@simonandschuster.com.
The Simon & Schuster Speakers Bureau can bring authors to your live event. For more information or to book an event contact the Simon & Schuster Speakers Bureau at 1-866-248-3049 or visit our website at www.simonspeakers.com.
Text by Matthew J. Gilbert
Designed by Hannah Frece
The text of this book was set in Causten Round.
Manufactured in the United States of America 1024 LAK
10 9 8 7 6 5 4 3 2 1
Library of Congress Cataloging-in-Publication Data
Names: Nonamus, Andy, author. | Jindra, Amy, illustrator.
Title: Go for the gold / by Andy Nonamus ; illustrated by Amy Jindra.
Description: First Little Simon paperback edition. | New York : Little Simon, 2024. | Series: The very worst ever ; 6 | Audience term: Children | Summary: A lucky coin causes an uncoordinated kid and an all-star athlete to swap skills in gym class.
Identifiers: LCCN 2024019749 (print) | LCCN 2024019750 (ebook) | ISBN 9781665959520 (paperback) | ISBN 9781665959537 (hardcover) | ISBN 9781665959544 (ebook)
Subjects: CYAC: Luck–Fiction. | Ability–Fiction. | Schools–Fiction. | Best friends–Fiction. | Friendship–Fiction.
Classification: LCC PZ7.1.N6378 Go 2024 (print) | LCC PZ7.1.N6378 (ebook) | DDC [Fic]–dc23
LC record available at https://lccn.loc.gov/2024019749
LC ebook record available at https://lccn.loc.gov/2024019750

CONTENTS

INTRODUCTION LETTER

CHAPTER 1	HIDE-AND-SCOOT	1
CHAPTER 2	HOME SWEET GYM	13
CHAPTER 3	THE GOLDS AND GRANOLA	27
CHAPTER 4	COIN TOSS	39
CHAPTER 5	TALLER, STRONGER, SMELLIER!	57
CHAPTER 6	GAME OFF!	73
CHAPTER 7	S'NOT SO GOOD	81
CHAPTER 8	TIME OUT!	93
CHAPTER 9	POINTS TAKEN	101
CHAPTER 10	BETTER THAN WINNING	109

Hey, Reader!

Thanks for checking out my story. Though I gotta warn you, I can't ever let you know my real name or what I look like. This may seem weird, but trust me, it's very important that I stay a secret.

Why? To protect myself! Seriously, these stories are super embarrassing!

Plus, you might even know me already! I could be in your class, on your baseball team, in your ballet class, or playing the tuba in your school band... anywhere!

Hi!

For all you know I could be sitting next to you right now!

So I went ahead and scratched out my name and put a sticker on my face, so you don't have to. You're welcome.

Now, we can both enjoy reading all about my awkward life . . . if you're into that kind of thing.

Peace out!
~~██████~~

1

HIDE-AND-SCOOT

I want you to imagine the scariest place ever.

Is it a vampire's castle? Or maybe a shark-infested volcano? Or worse yet . . . a vampire's castle inside a shark-infested volcano?!

Pffft!

I was in an even worse place.

Here, it smelled like moldy sneakers. Kids charged at you from all corners. Books fell from shelves and tripped you.

I'm talking about . . . *the Library-Gym.*

(Yeah, you read that right. It's the library *and* the gym.)

My class was in the last round of scooter soccer practice. It's as wacky as it sounds. You hop on a scooter, wheel around, and kick the ball into the right net.

And me? I wasn't playing, I was hiding. But I wasn't alone. I'd met two new friends—Shiny Coin and Dust Bunny.

Don't judge me for not playing. It's much safer for everyone this way.

Remember when I tried boomerang tag? The whole school lost working lights for weeks.

FWEEET! went Coach Olympia's whistle, and I flinched at the sound.

Peeking from my hiding spot, I saw her standing on one of the library tables. She might look sweet, but Coach Olympia didn't mess around.

"You call that scootin'?" she shouted at the players. "That won't win the after-school scooter soccer tournament! Look at Jake Gold—*he's* got what it takes."

Jake swooshed past me, did a cool backflip on his scooter, and kicked the ball into the net. He was one of my best friends and one of the best kids in gym. His parents were athletes, after all.

"SCORE!" his team cheered.

"Go, Jake!" I whisper-cheered.

They were doing just fine without me. But then something terrible happened.

Jake looked my way.

"What are you doing back there?" he asked. "The game is over here, silly!"

Now everyone looked my way. And Coach did *not* look happy.

"▒▒▒▒▒▒!" she shouted. "Get back in the game and stop cheating!"

"I'm not cheating at scooter soccer," I squealed. "I'm *hiding* from it."

"No excuses!" she shouted. "You just cost your team two points."

DING! The scoreboard subtracted two points from my side.

"Dude!" a kid complained. "How could you?"

"So long, Shiny Coin," I said. "So long, Dust Bunny. Hello, helmet."

Grabbing my scooter from the ground, I kicked off. But instead of moving forward, my scooter moved backward.

Coach Olympia said, "Yikes! I mean, keep trying!"

I did keep trying . . . and rolled right into a stash of overdue books.

"Ugh," I groaned. "I . . . can't . . . do. . . this."

"I've got you, bro!" Jake shouted from across the room.

He pushed off his scooter and made the coolest spin turn ever toward me.

"You just need some riding lessons!" Jake said, helping me up. "Practice at my house later?"

Oh, great. Just what I wanted.

2

HOME SWEET GYM

Jake and I waited for our two other best friends after school.

Regina du Lar usually gave us a ride home in her fancy limo. She was mega rich and mega cool.

Then there was Glinda Alegre. She was gloomy, but also secretly nice.

Don't tell her I said that.

After a few minutes, though, I didn't see either of them.

Did we get stood up?

"I wonder where Regina and Glinda are," I said as I looked around.

"Oh, they're not coming!" Jake said. "I told them to go on without us."

I frowned. "Why?"

Then Jake gave me a look that I really didn't like. It was a look that made me start to sweat. This was his competition look.

He started to run in place.

"Oh no," I said, backing away. "You don't mean..."

"We're going to run home!" he said.

"Now, come on before they release the after-school guard dogs."

I gulped.

Jake ran all the way home.

Me? Sure, I ran. But then I slowed down to a jog. And then I walked.

By the time Jake turned into his driveway, I was crawling on my hands and knees like a baby.

"Here we are, bro!" Jake called out. "Home sweet home!"

Slowly, I raised my head to take a look. "Whaaa...?"

Some people have a home gym where they like to exercise.

But the Golds? They had a gym that was a *home*.

I couldn't believe my eyes. From the outside, the house was three stories tall. There was a track that went all the way around it like an exercise moat! There was even a rock-climbing wall built into it. And I'm pretty sure you could bungee jump from the roof.

I couldn't find the right words to say how scary this place was for me.

"Pretty cool, huh?" Jake laughed. "Come on!"

I was so tired, I let him drag me across the front yard.

But the nightmare wasn't over. Because every nightmare needs a monster. As soon as we stepped inside the house, a jingling sound echoed down the hall.

"Um, what's that noise?" I asked.

"Oooh, that's Coach!" Jake said.

"You hired a coach just to help me learn scooter soccer?" I asked.

Jake shook his head. "Nah. He lives here. And it's time for his snack."

"What does he like?" I asked. "Protein shakes?"

"No, silly," Jake replied. "He eats bones!"

"Bones?!" I cried out. "What kind of coach eats bones?!"

A large shadow stretched along the hallway. I saw sharp teeth, slobber dripping down from its mouth, and giant legs. Then the thing jumped from around the corner and right at me!

"GAH!" I shouted. "IT'S LICKING ME!"

Jake laughed. "That's just how coach says hello."

I peeked open an eye and was happily surprised to see a tiny Chihuahua.

"Oh!" I said with a huge sigh of relief. "I didn't know you had a dog!"

"He's not my *dog*," Jake said. "He's my coach."

Before I could ask more questions, a voice from somewhere in the house called, "Is that my Jakey I hear?"

THE GOLDS AND GRANOLA

Thankfully, scooter soccer practice didn't start right away.

First, I had to meet the Golds.

"It smells like the winner of this year's scooter soccer tournament has arrived!" Mr. Gold's voice boomed. "And there's also something stinky I can't quite place...."

I smelled my armpits. Could they smell me coming?!

When we entered the living room, the TV was on the sports channel, but no one was watching.

"Hi, Mom! Hi, Dad!" Jake said.

That's when I noticed Jake was looking up.

I looked up too.

Mr. and Mrs. Gold were rock climbing on the ceiling. Now that I was paying closer attention, I realized the entire living room was a rock-climbing gym!

"Oh! You must be ▬▬▬▬!" said Mrs. Gold as she sprang toward the next hold. "Jake's told us so much about you. Climb on up here and say hello!"

"Um, thanks, but I like it better here on the ground," I said.

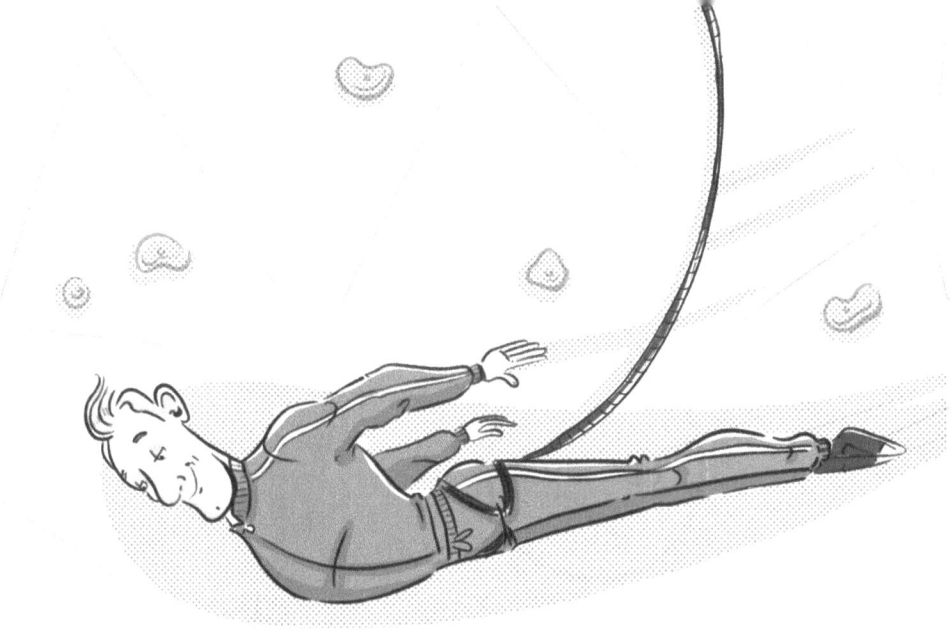

Mr. Gold soared across the room. "Sorry you've caught us like this. We're relaxing after a very long day of training for the Triple Threat Trial."

I couldn't imagine ever relaxing by rock climbing on the ceiling.

"The Triple Threat Trial?" I asked.

"It's an event they created," Jake explained. "They swim for three miles, run underwater for three hours, and bike nonstop on land for three days."

"It's too easy, we know." Mr. Gold hopped down to meet us.

It didn't sound easy to me.

"Wow, you know, I can't even dog-paddle," I answered honestly.

Mrs. Gold dropped down next to her husband and laughed. "Oh, you're funny! Laughter is good exercise. How about we fuel those muscles with snacks?"

Finally, I thought. Maybe I could impress Jake's parents with how much food I could scarf down! If there was ever an event I could win, it was probably an eating contest. Okay, maybe a burping contest too.

My mouth watered as Mrs. Gold pulled a tray of freshly baked granola bars out of the oven.

"Each bar has a different flavor," she explained. "Purple is prune, green is broccoli, and—"

"Oooh! I'll try this one!" I said, reaching for one with chocolate chips. I took a big bite and immediately regretted it. "Um ... whaaizzthis?"

"That's the kidney bean bar," Jake answered. "Yummy!"

"Y-yeah," I said, making myself swallow it down.

I was saved by the sudden sound of FWEEEET!

It was Coach, blowing a tiny whistle on his collar.

"You heard Coach," Jake cheered. "Practice time!"

Hmm, maybe I wasn't safe yet.

COIN TOSS

Remember how I said that this house was my nightmare? Well, it was every athlete's dream.

The dream continued on the way to Jake's room. The walls were lined with all sorts of trophies and medals.

Jake pointed out a few as we walked along.

"Dad won this trophy for typing the fastest. This one was Mom's first Swan Song Skydiving trophy," said Jake. "She sang the entire way down!"

A medal with Jake's face caught my eye. "What's this one for?"

Jake removed his cap and swished his golden hair. "That's the first-place award for softest hair."

I had to give it to Jake. His hair was amazing.

With his cap back on, Jake led us to a room with a golden plate on the door. It read:

JAKE GOLD STADIUM

"There's a stadium named after you?" I asked.

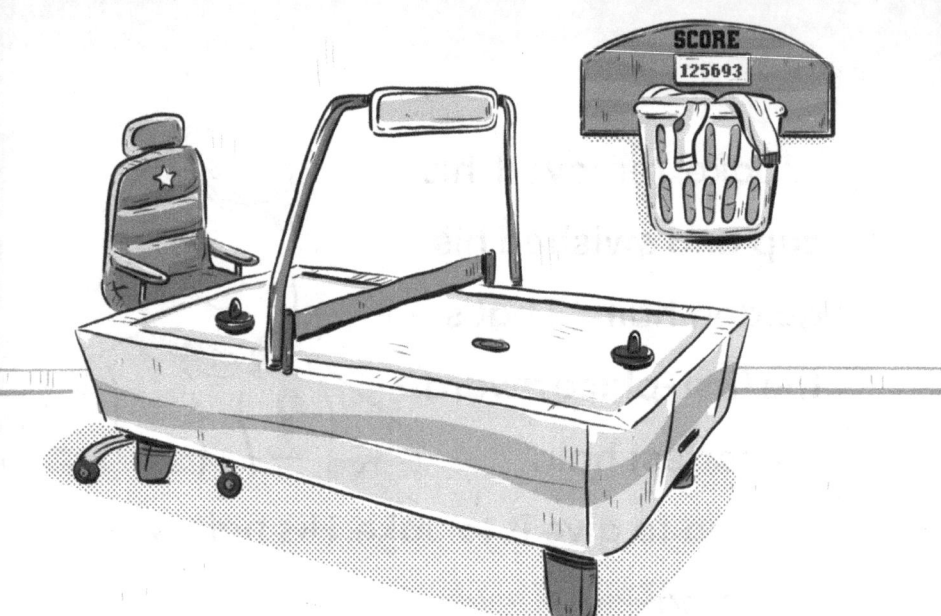

"Yes," Jake replied. "But this is the smaller version—my room!"

When he opened the door, we were hit by flashing lights and loud music. While the rest of the house was a gym, Jake's bedroom was like an arcade.

His desk? It was also an air hockey table!

His bed? It was a king-sized ball pit. You had to *dig* for pillows.

And his laundry basket? It was on the wall and had its own scoreboard.

Plus the room was covered in trophies and medals—all gold.

Jake peeled off his dirty socks and slam-dunked them into the basket.

"NOTHIN' BUT NET!" the scoreboard said in a robotic voice. "GO, GOLD!"

"You even put your dirty laundry away like a champ," I said. "Let me try."

I took off one sock, squatted down, and then hopped up to toss it in. Just as it reached the net, the sock bounced off the rim and fell back into my face.

"Yuck!" I cried out. Man, I really *did* stink.

The scoreboard made a sad sound. "WOMP, WOMP! YOU NEED PRACTICE!"

Jake opened his closet. "That's why we're here! The after-school scooter soccer tournament is no joke. Coach Olympia expects us to try our best, and I plan on winning every round!"

Wait, *every round* . . . how many games were in this silly tournament?

"There's a court we can practice on upstairs," Jake said. "You ready?"

Suddenly I became nervous again. It's not that I didn't trust Jake to help me. It's just that I knew I wouldn't be good. What if I disappointed him?

"I need a potty break first," I said quickly. "Where's your bathroom?"

I didn't *really* need to go to the bathroom. But I was feeling a little queasy with all this sports talk.

I rushed out of Jake's room and found ... um ... this place?

It had a toilet and a shower, but it also had a massage table and disco balls.

But I wasn't here to worry about how much Jake danced in the shower. I was here to worry about me!

I walked over to the mirror and whispered, "Please, please, *please* be good at this!"

"*Psst!* Hey!" a voice suddenly said.

I looked around, startled. "Um, I should be the only person in this room, but ... hello?"

"In your pocket!" the voice said again.

I dug into my pocket and found something small and round. It was Shiny Coin!

"How'd you get in here?" I gasped. "I thought I left you at school."

"I'm not just *any* coin," it said. "I'm a magic *lucky* coin. Lucky enough to help even you!"

"How?" I asked.

"Just make a wish and toss me into the toilet," it explained.

I peeked over at the bowl and frowned. "I thought you needed a wishing well for wishes."

"Eh, water's water," the coin replied.

I thought it over. *What if I'm just getting my hopes up? What if I'm seeing things? What if I'm talking to a regular, nonmagic coin? Does anyone talk to coins? Do the coins talk back to them?*

But what if ... this worked?

Holding the coin close to my heart, I made my wish.

"Please make me good at sports," I said. "No matter the cost!"

Then I flicked it into the toilet. The coin flipped slowly through the air and I had a new thought.

Maybe making a wish by tossing a coin into my best friend's toilet wasn't the best idea.

But then... *SPLASH!*

It could have been my imagination, but I started to feel a little different.

(Or maybe it was just the kidney bean bar.)

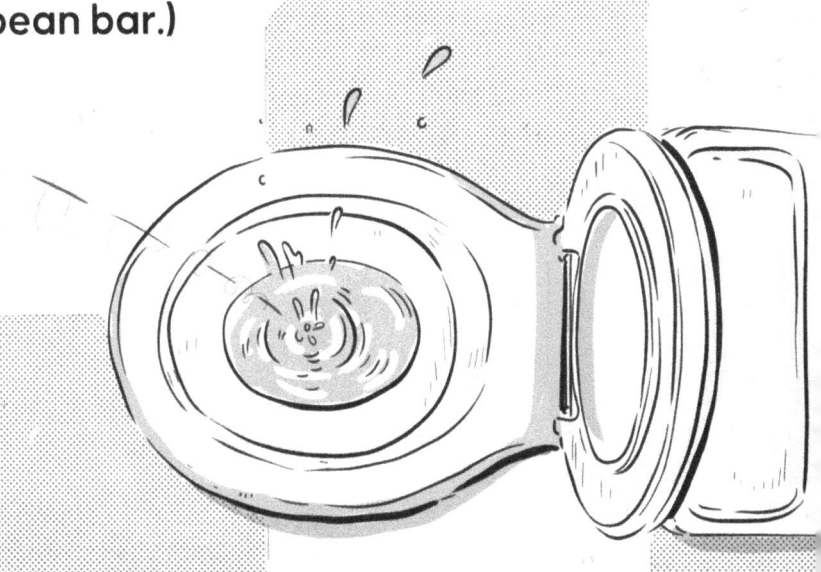

5

TALLER, STRONGER, SMELLIER!

We knew it was time for the first tournament game when Coach Olympia took the soccer nets outside.

Teachers, parents, and students sat in the bleachers. I don't know why they were excited to be there. I wasn't.

We were kids, on scooters, trying to kick a soccer ball. It was barely a sport.

But that didn't matter to the fans. They brought popcorn and snacks. They even had posters and banners. One giant banner announced:

THE AFTER-SCHOOL SCOOTER SOCCER TOURNAMENT BEGINS TODAY! COME SEE CLASS 312 AND CLASS 4 FACE OFF!

I wished it said something like this instead:

MATCH CANCELED. SPORTS ARE BANNED FOREVER!

Jake appeared at my side. He looked at the banner and smiled. "We're playing class 4 first? Easy!"

"But isn't class 4 all the stronger, older kids?" I asked.

Jake waved a hand. "They're not *that* big."

WHAM! The school doors burst open and out came class 4.

"Come on over, kiddos!" Coach Olympia shouted.

Except those kiddos didn't look like "kiddos." They were tall. They were strong. And they looked ready to win.

A kid with a unibrow shouted, "Prepare to be crushed like a soda can!"

I felt like I was going to be sick.

Over by the bleachers, Coach Olympia blew her whistle. "Welcome to the first round of the scooter soccer tournament! Remember to play by the rules. Any questions?"

I raised my hand. "Do I *have* to play?"

"Yes!" she shouted, then blew her whistle again. "Get in position!"

Grumbling, I followed my class to one side of the court. We grabbed our scooters, hopped on, and held on tight to the handles. The class 4 kids were so big, the scooters looked teeny tiny.

"On your marks, get set, SCOOT LIKE YOUR LIFE DEPENDS ON IT!" shouted Coach Olympia.

FWEET! It was game on.

Everyone wheeled into action. I tried to kick off, but a kid bumped into me. I went spinning across the court.

"WAAAAHHHHH!" I shouted.

"Watch where you're scootin'!" someone from class 4 said as he shoved me.

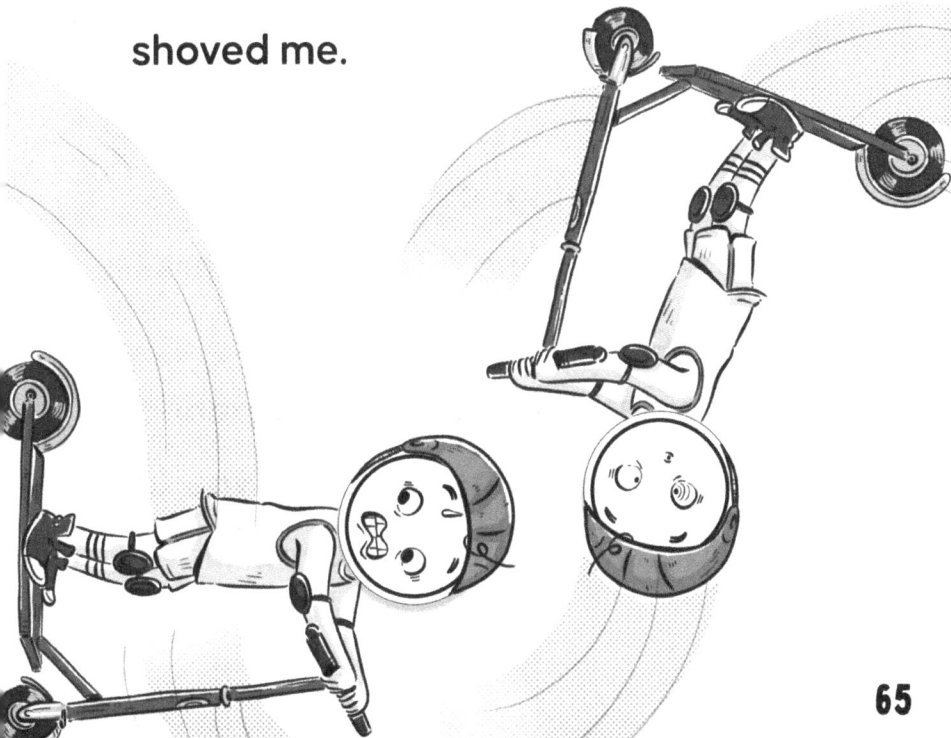

I went soaring over the players. Where would I land? The bleachers? Another town?

But something strange happened instead. My spinning scooter was in midair, and so was the soccer ball.

But there was a piece of gum on the bottom of my shoe! It stuck to the ball and the ball stuck to me.

I kicked and kicked until the ball finally flew away.

That's when I heard a loud *DING*!

"One point for class 312!" Coach shouted.

"Wait, what?" I said. "Did I score?"

Everyone was silent for a moment. Then Jake shouted, "YOU DID!"

The crowd went wild. My team swarmed around me. I couldn't believe it! And here's something you won't believe... I *kept* scoring points! It was like I couldn't miss!

I kicked the ball from the ground, from a swing, and even while I was taking a water break. Even when I wasn't trying, I still scored.

DING!

DING!

DING!

We won the first game, and everyone was cheering my name. "▬▬▬! ▬▬▬! ▬▬▬!"

"Congrats, kid," Coach Olympia said. "You're the only player who scored today."

"Whoa, dude," Jake said. "It was like the ball only went to you. How did you do that?"

"I don't know!" I admitted. "I guess I'm better at this than I thought!"

GAME OFF!

After my big victory, every day felt like a win.

During class, I knew the answers. When I played video games, I beat the highest scores. I just couldn't lose.

It wasn't until class the next day that I noticed something was off about my luck.

It all started when our teacher, Mr. Hughes, called Jake's name.

Instead of leaping up, though, Jake stayed slumped at his desk.

"Can you hear me, Mr. Gold?" asked Mr. Hughes.

"My name's not Jake Gold anymore," mumbled Jake. "*Gold* means 'number one.' *Gold* means 'winner.' You can just call me ... Jake *Silver*."

Mr. Hughes raised his eyebrow. "All right, Mr. Silver. Can you pass out papers, please?"

Jake got up. But the minute he took a step, he tripped over his own shoelaces and tumbled in front of the whole class! Papers went flying everywhere!

To make things worse, everyone laughed... even Mr. Hughes!

Jake looked totally horrified.

I knew that look.

It was the look of someone who had embarrassed himself. It was the look that was usually on my face.

Everything went downhill for Jake after that.

Instead of getting an A on a sports quiz, he got a B.

Instead of being chosen first to answer a question, he was chosen second.

The lunch ladies served him the most burnt square of pizza in the cafeteria. But it was at recess that something really bad happened.

Jake wasn't the first player picked for basketball. I was.

And guess what? I was great!

I made every basket, but Jake, well, he just couldn't win.

He looked down at his hands.

"I can't shoot the ball, I can't pass the ball, I can't even pass out papers! What's wrong with me?!" Jake cried out in horror. "I feel like I've been cursed!"

Jake took off his hat and I gasped at the terrible sight.

His swishy golden hair wasn't so perfect anymore. It was suddenly flattened out and stuck to his head, all greasy and damp.

Jake Gold—the golden star—had lost his shine.

S'NOT SO GOOD

But surely Jake would shine again at our second scooter soccer game. This time we were playing class 10, and they were the youngest class.

They were shorter, wimpier, and smelled like stinky diapers. The team captain had snot dripping out of his nose. (Well, they all did.)

"We're going to wipe the floor with you!" he said, the snot drooping lower.

"Maybe try wiping your nose first?" I suggested.

"Ha, yeah!" Jake said. "Because . . . because there's *snot* in it!"

Wow. Even his trash talk was bad.

Coach Olympia marched out to start the match. But before she blew her whistle, she made a big announcement.

"We're raising the stakes for this round," she said. "Because today's winning class will get to skip gym... FOR TWO WHOLE WEEKS!"

Everyone watching from the bleachers erupted into applause. I burst into excited screaming.

Forget shiny talking coins. This was a truly priceless treasure!

I strapped on my helmet and narrowed my eyes. "All right, class 312. We've got this one in the bag!"

"Yeah!" they shouted.

"Y-yeah!" Jake said, a bit too late.

"Get into your positions!" Coach Olympia said.

We all hurried to our spots. The second I heard the whistle, I kick-flipped into action.

DING! DING! DING! I scored three points right away.

The snotty-nosed kid had the ball next, but I stole it from him and scored. "You'll regret that!" he shouted.

He pressed a finger to his nose and shot a snot rocket.

The sticky boogers swung toward me, but I ducked. They hit Jake right in the face.

I scored another point by accidentally kicking the ball into the stands. It bounced off Mr. Hughes's head, popped through a snot bubble, and flew into the net.

"Stop scoring so many points!" cried a teensy player from class 10.

"You a *little* mad?" I teased.

Then I scored again.

As for Jake, I wanted to pass to him, but he wasn't anywhere on the court. Nope, he was on the sideline. His scooter had lost a wheel, and he was covered in snot.

"Why is this happening to me?" he shouted.

But nobody heard him because they were all cheering for me!

"GO, ▬▬▬ GOLD!"
"GO, ▬▬▬ GOLD!"

They were calling me by Jake's last name! I had become the school's *new Gold*. And the real Jake Gold didn't like that one bit.

"But . . . but . . . *I'm* supposed to be the real Gold!" he cried out.

Jake tried to run off the field, but he slipped on a green snot puddle and was covered in oozy goo.

It was so gross that it made the entire crowd gag.

Things were *snot* going Jake's way. *S'not* at all.

TIME OUT!

"Time out!" I said as I ran after Jake.

I found him sitting by the water fountain. He was a little cleaner from the snot, but still dripping wet.

I sat beside him on the floor and slopped my hand on his wet shoulder.

"Do I want to know why you are soaked?" I asked

"I tried to wash off in the water fountain, but the fountain threw up all over me," Jake cried. "I can't even clean myself up without making a mess."

Poor guy. He was sad, and wet, and covered in someone else's boogers.

But I was the one who needed to come clean.

"Jake, I have to tell you something. What's happening to you is *my* fault," I admitted. "I made a wish on a magic coin, and I threw it into your toilet like it was a wishing well."

"That explains why our toilet overflowed after you left," Jake said. "I thought it was from all the broccoli bars I ate."

I sighed. "Don't blame the broccoli. My wish made us swap places! I got your skills, and you got my bad luck. And all because I wished to be better at sports. I don't even like sports, I just didn't want to let anyone down."

"But you could never let us down!" he cried. "You're the greatest friend."

I smiled. "Thanks, bud. Maybe we can find another lucky coin and I can fix this."

Jake paused. "You would give all this up . . . for me?"

"Sure. You're my best friend," I said. "Whether you win or not."

Jake gave me a very big, very wet hug. It was sweet, but also pretty snotty.

"Thanks, bro," Jake said. "But it's gonna take more than toilet-wish magic to help me get back in the game. Besides, we've always made a great team. Maybe we just have to play this game *our* way."

I held out my fist for a best-friend bump, and boy was it powerful.

I felt a wild charge.

Something was different now. Something had changed. I just couldn't figure out what.

POINTS TAKEN

Jake and I returned to a hero's welcome ... from the other team.

"You see?" I said. "They love you!"

Jake frowned. "Um, class 10 is cheering at us, not for us."

I looked toward those little kids and saw that Jake was right. Class 10 acted like they were winning!

"What are *you* guys happy about?" I asked.

The booger captain smiled and said, "Just check out the scoreboard!"

When I left to check on Jake, we had a six-point lead. But now? It was totally different!

"There's been some kind of mistake!" I shouted. "They took our points!"

"No mistake," Coach Olympia explained. "Those points have been rightfully taken."

"Why?" I groaned, and dropped to the ground.

Coach Olympia tossed a roll of paper at me. I luckily caught it before it could slam into my face. The scroll glittered, as if made of magic.

"Whoa," Jake whispered, his eyes glowing. "Is that what I think it is?"

I let the scroll fall open. It was so long, I couldn't hold it all by myself.

It was titled SCOOTER SOCCER OFFICIAL RULES.

"As you can see here, Rule 412, Article 5, clearly states that leaving the game to sit by the water fountain is against the rules," Coach explained. "All your points are taken away and given to the other team."

I slumped. "That's a terrible rule!"

"True," Coach Olympia said. "That's probably why no one's bothered to break it before. Except you."

I looked around at my team, seeing nothing but disappointed faces.

For a moment, I felt like giving up.

But then Jake grabbed me by the shoulders and shook me. "Those points will be easy-breezy to earn back! We just need a game plan."

He shook me over and over, and a plan began forming in my head.

"Keep shaking me!" I shouted as I had a lightbulb idea.

I remembered the practice shot I took in Jake's room. I had thrown in a sock and it had bounced off.

Not because I was bad at sports. But because I'd been distracted by how nervous I was.

To win this match, I didn't need to be the best or luckiest player.

I just had to be the best *distraction*.

10

BETTER THAN WINNING

FWEET!

The game was back on.

The ball bounced this way and that, from player to player. It wasn't long before I saw the ball soaring straight to me. All the Class 10 players scootered my way in a swarm.

"Get him!" they screamed.

As the ball bounced closer and closer, my hands tingled with invisible luck. I could almost hear the voice of the talking coin in my head. It said, *Dude, I'm giving you magical luck! Do you think I went swimming in the toilet for nothing?*

But I had my own wild plan.

Holding on tight to the scooter handles, I kicked off and flew right into the water coolers. *Blammo!* Ice flew everywhere. Somehow, I lost a sock, too.

It was classic me!

Class 10 stared at me, confused. None of them noticed an open soccer net behind them. Not a single one noticed that no one was blocking it!

But Jake Gold? Yeah, he noticed.

He did what the Golds do best—he moved to win!

"You've lost your lucky spark!" the class 10 captain teased.

"And thank goodness for that!" I said. "Because I made you look."

The kid tilted his head. His snot drooped down farther. "Huh?"

I lay on the ground and said, "That's what we call a 'distraction.'"

DING-DING-DING!
Jake Gold scored!
The crowd roared.
"Go, JAKE GOLD!"
"Go, JAKE GOLD!"

"JAKE GOLD IS BACK!" Jake cried out, holding up his scooter.

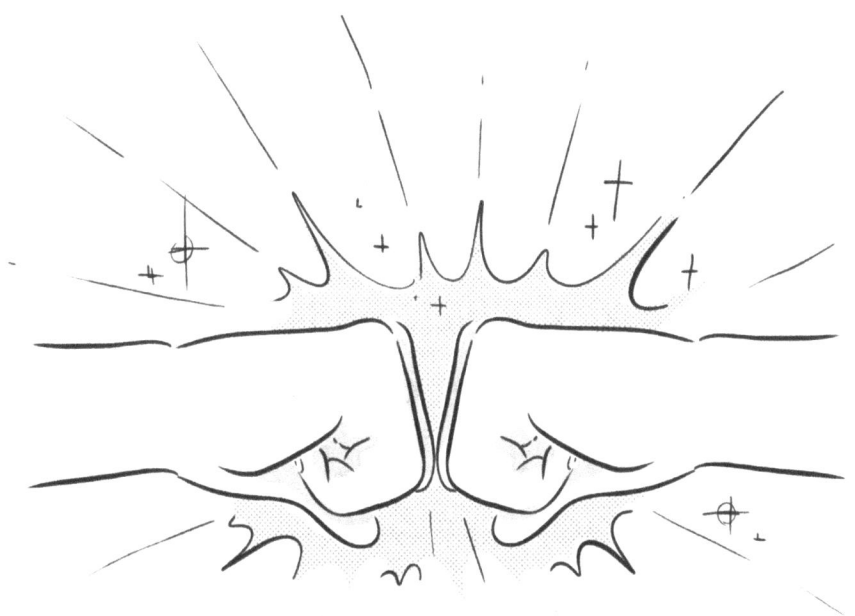

"Nice, bro!" I said, giving him a fist bump.

"Couldn't have done it without you," he said. "Now let's go win!"

And so we played on. Jake Gold couldn't stop scoring after that.

I tripped, slipped, and dipped into all the wrong corners of the court.

Meanwhile, Jake scored, scored, and scored. He even did his famous backflip-kick, which made the crowd applaud and break out into a chant.

"LET'S GO, JAKE GOLD!"

"LET'S GO, JAKE GOLD!"

Maybe I should've been a little bit embarrassed by the way I played.

I mean, I did get the worst penalty in the game, lost us six points, and crashed my scooter in front of the whole school.

But you know what? I was glad to be me again.

It felt better than winning.

HERE'S A PEEK AT ▓▓▓▓▓▓▓'S NEXT ADVENTURE!

According to the banner across the school doors, today was going to be a big day.

See?

TODAY'S GOING TO BE BIG, KID!

And banners don't lie, right?

So I walked through the school

An excerpt from *Backstage Fright*

hallway and saw a smaller banner. This one read:

> FIND OUT MORE AT THE BIG ASSEMBLY WITH A BIG SURPRISE!

And when I reached the auditorium doors, I had to squint to read the tiniest banner yet.

> ALSO, YOUR SHOE'S UNTIED. . . .

"'Your . . . shoe's . . . untied?'" I read aloud.

I took a step forward, trying to see if maybe I'd read that last bit wrong.

But no, I hadn't. I quickly found out that my shoelaces *were* untied, and I tripped.

An excerpt from *Backstage Fright*

To make things worse, I was diving headfirst into a stinky, goopy, pile of ... whatever that is.

Gum? Slime? Moldy cheese? I just couldn't tell!

While this is super embarrassing, don't feel too bad for me. Unlucky things like this happen to me all the time. My middle name might as well be Bad Luck.

Sometimes dogs chase me when I'm covered in delicious breakfast syrup.

Other times I accidentally cause a popcorn tidal wave during a school carnival.

An excerpt from *Backstage Fright*